1

The Sugar Creek Gang was having one of the most exciting, adventurous summers ever. When we killed the fierce, savage-tempered, twenty-eight-toothed wildcat, we never dreamed that the very next week we'd have a hair-raising experience in a haunted house.

It had been quite a while since the gang had visited the haunted house, far up in the hills above Old Man Paddler's cabin. In fact, we hadn't visited Old Man Paddler himself for some time. And in a way, that kind, long-whiskered old man was responsible for our running into the brand-new, very dangerous, haunted-house mystery.

Big Jim, the leader of our gang, had seen the old man that morning and had an important story to tell us when the gang met the afternoon of that ordinary day—ordinary, that is, until we heard what Big Jim had to tell us.

The part of the story that had to do with me, Bill Collins, started at our house. That's because it was very important that I get to go to the gang meeting down by the swimming hole, and whether or not I could go depended, as it usually does, on Mom or Dad or both.

It also depended on me. And on that day I wasn't very dependable. My parents didn't think so, anyway. It never feels good to be on the outs with your parents when it's your own fault, and they seemed to think it was my fault.

Dragonfly, the crooked-nosed, allergy-pestered member of our gang was going to start on an out-West vacation the very next week to get away from the ragweed pollen, which always gave him hay fever and asthma. His folks had bought him a pair of beautiful cowboy boots and a very fancy broad-brimmed Stetson cowboy hat.

Now, I had saved money that summer toward a new suit I would need in the fall, but I had decided that I needed a pair of cowboy boots and a cowboy hat worse—a whole lot worse. And I was sure that I needed them right now.

Both Mom and Dad had said no and meant it the first time. But I wanted that hat and those boots so much that I thought it was worth taking a chance on getting into trouble. That very week I'd said in a tone of voice that my parents called fussy, "Dragonfly's parents like their son. They want him to look like a Westerner. My parents want me to wear overalls and go barefoot and stay home!"

I had to miss my supper dessert that day and go to bed without getting to listen to the Lone Ranger program.

That was pretty hard on me because for a week or more I myself had been the Lone Ranger. I rode my big white stallion, Silver, over our farm and up and down the creek, cap-

34

SUGAR CREEK GANG

LOCKED IN THE ATTIC

Paul Hutchens

MOODY PRESS

CHICAGO

Original Title: *Down a Sugar Creek Gang Chimney*

ISBN: 0-8024-7039-4

3 5 7 9 10 8 6 4 2

Printed in the United States of America

PREFACE

Hi—from a member of the Sugar Creek Gang!

It's just that I don't know which one I am. When I was good, I was Little Jim. When I did bad things—well, sometimes I was Bill Collins or even mischievous Poetry.

You see, I am the daughter of Paul Hutchens, and I spent many an hour listening to him read his manuscript as far as he had written it that particular day. I went along to the north woods of Minnesota, to Colorado, and to the various other places he would go to find something different for the Gang to do.

Now the years have passed—more than fifty, actually. My father is in heaven, but the Gang goes on. All thirty-six books are still in print and now are being updated for today's readers with input from my five children, who also span the decades from the '50s to the '70s.

The real Sugar Creek is in Indiana, and my father and his six brothers were the original Gang. But the idea of the books and their ministry were and are the Lord's. It is He who keeps the Gang going.

PAULINE HUTCHENS WILSON

turing rustlers, saving stagecoach passengers from getting robbed, bringing law and order to the whole territory, and ordering around my imaginary faithful Indian companion, Tonto, as if he was a real person.

It seemed that Dragonfly was to blame for my half-mad spell even more than my parents. If he hadn't been wearing his fancy boots and his swept-brim hat, I wouldn't have wanted a hat and a pair of boots like them. I was mad at my folks, but I was madder at Dragonfly.

The weather that day was hot, hot, hot. The sun poured down yellow heat all over everything and everybody, making all our tempers quick, our muscles lazy, and our minds—mine especially—a little more stubborn.

Every few minutes that sultry morning, a whirlwind would spiral from the direction of the south pasture, sweep across the barnyard, and lose itself in the cornfield. Whenever I could, if the stormy little spiral came anywhere near where I was working—or was supposed to be working—I'd leave whatever I was doing, make a barefoot beeline for it, toss myself into it, and go zigzagging along with it whichever way it went. Sometimes it seemed to go in every direction at the same time.

One of the most pleasant experiences a boy ever has is to go racing and dodging along, trying to stay in the eye of a whirlwind, enjoying the wind fanning his face. Sometimes I get dust in my eyes and can't see and have to let the happy little spiral go whirling on without me.

The gang meeting was supposed to be at half past one that afternoon in the shade of the Snatzerpazooka Tree. That's the little river birch that grows at the edge of Dragonfly's father's cornfield near the sandy beach of our swimming hole. We had named that friendly little river birch Snatzerpazooka right after we'd had a Western-style necktie party there and strung up a ridiculous-looking scarecrow from its overhanging branch to keep the crows from eating up the new shoots of corn. Snatzerpazooka was the name we'd given the scarecrow.

I was surprised at how easy it was for me to leave our house that afternoon without having to do the dishes. I am maybe one of the best dishwashers and dryers in the whole neighborhood from having had so much experience doing them. Sometimes I even do them without being told to.

"Run along to your meeting," Dad ordered me from under his reddish brown mustache. "Your mother and I have some important things to discuss. Things you might not be interested in." Dad's right eye winked in Mom's direction.

I couldn't let myself worry about whether or not they really wanted me to stay and help with the dishes and were just pretending they didn't. It looked like a good time to be excused from the table and get started for the Snatzerpazooka Tree.

Pretty soon I was just outside the east screen

door, going kind of slowly, since it would be easier to be stopped if I wasn't going so fast.

"Hi, there!" I said to Mixy, our black-and-white house cat, stooping to give her a few friendly strokes just as I heard Dad say to Mom, "It didn't work that time."

Her answer wasn't easy to hear, because the radio with the noon news program was on in the living room and my mind was listening to both at the same time.

The newscaster was racing along about somebody who had escaped from jail somewhere. He was armed and should be considered extremely dangerous. I didn't pay much attention, because it was the kind of news we were getting used to. Whoever the fugitive from justice was, he wouldn't be anybody around Sugar Creek. And besides, whoever he was, the jail he had broken out of was probably a long way from here.

Hearing the news did give me an idea, though. Dad's order to run along to the meeting was like unlocking the Collins family jail and letting his boy out.

In a few minutes my bare feet had carried me past the hammock swinging under the plum tree and all the way across the grassy lawn to the high rope swing under the walnut tree near the front gate and our mailbox.

It was too early to meet the gang. It was also too hot to run, and I was half angry at my folks for wanting me gone so they could talk about something I wasn't supposed to hear. Besides, any minute now they might wake up to the fact that their prisoner had escaped, and Dad's voice would sail out across the yard, lasso me, and drag me back. I might as well hang around a while and wait for his gruff-voiced lariat to come flying through the air with the greatest of ease.

In a flash I was standing on the board seat of the swing, pumping myself higher and higher before sitting down to "let the old cat die." That is what a boy does when he quits pumping and lets the swing coast to a stop by itself.

While I was enjoying the breeze in my face, the flapping of my shirt sleeves, and the rush of wind in my ears, I was quoting to myself a poem we had learned in school. It was by Robert Louis Stevenson, who had also written *Treasure Island*.

> *How do you like to go up in a swing,*
> *Up in the air so blue?*
> *Oh, I do think it the pleasantest thing*
> *Ever a child can do!*

I was still letting the old cat die—it was half dead already—and my voice was singsonging along on the second stanza of the poem, when I was interrupted by a long-tailed sneeze not far away.

I knew whose sneeze it was. There wasn't another boy in the world that could sneeze like that. Only Dragonfly Roy Gilbert could do it. Anytime, any day, anywhere around Sugar Creek you could expect to hear him let out a long-tailed sneeze with some ridiculous word or half-dozen words mixed up in it. One of his favorite sneezes was "Kersnatzerpazooka!"

Dragonfly was especially proud of his sneezing, except in hay fever season, when he had to do too much of it. This summer, though, as you already know, he was going to the Rockies to get away from ragweed pollen.

Maybe I ought to tell you that being interrupted is one of my pet peeves. I don't like having my thoughts interrupted when I'm in my world of imagination, dreaming about something a boy likes to dream about. In fact, it's sometimes a lot more fun to dream about doing things than it is to actually do them.

I certainly didn't enjoy being exploded back into such an ordinary world as it was that day, especially when I might get called in to do a stack of dishes. I wanted to go on swinging to the tune of the dying cat, quoting the poem all the way to its end. Just in case you've never read it or heard anybody read it, this is the way the rest of it goes.

Up in the air and over the wall,
Till I can see so wide,
Rivers and trees and cattle and all
Over the countryside—

Till I look down on the garden green,
Down on the roof so brown—
Up in the air I go flying again,
Up in the air and down!

As I said, Dragonfly's ridiculous sneeze interrupted me in the middle of the second stanza.

I looked in the direction it seemed the sneeze had come from and saw across the road, standing beside our washtub birdbath in the shade of the elderberry bush that grew there, a spindle-legged, crooked-nosed boy, Dragonfly himself. I could hardly see his face, though, for the broad-brimmed cowboy hat he was wearing. His jeans made his legs look even skinnier than they were, which is what jeans sometimes do to people.

Half angry because of the interruption and because of who it was, I started to yell out to him the rest of the verse I was in the middle of.

I didn't get very far, because he interrupted me again to boast, "I'm going to ride on the longest chairlift in the world when I get out West, clear up to the top of Ajax Mountain! We can look out over thousands of square miles of mountains! The people below us will look like ants and the cars like toy cars!"

"Oh yeah!" I yelled back across the dusty road to him. My dying cat came to life again as my temper and I both went higher and higher.

"Yeah!" he called back in a bragging voice.

It was the *way* he said what he said that stirred up my pet peeve, not just my being interrupted two or three times. I was used to all the members of the gang bragging a little, doing it just for fun, the way most boys do. But this seemed different. After all, he needn't act so uppity just because of his fancy boots and hat.

Besides, our rope swing was the highest in the whole Sugar Creek territory, and you could see a long way when you were up in the air on it!

"Hey!" I exclaimed to him all of a sudden. "*Don't empty out that water!* That's for the birds!"

I was really mad now. That washtub had been left there on purpose. I kept it filled with clean water for the birds to bathe in and for them to get their drinking water, so we'd have more birds in the neighborhood and they wouldn't have to fly way down to the spring or to the creek every time they were thirsty.

But do you know what? That sneezy little guy had swept off his wide-brimmed hat, plunged it into the tub of water, and lifted it out with its crown filled to the brim! "Here, Silver!" I heard him say. "Have a drink! You're plumb tuckered out after that wild ride across the prairie from Dodge!"

And in my mind I saw what was going on in his. He was imagining himself to be one of the most popular cowboys of the Old West, the Lone Ranger himself, and was giving his white horse, Silver, a drink.

Anybody who knows even a little about a Western cowboy probably knows that his hat and his boots are the most important part of his clothes. He's not too particular about what he wears between his head and his feet. He buys an extrafine hat with a stiff brim so it won't flop in his eyes in the wind and blind him when he is in danger. He chooses an extrawide brim so he'll have it for a sunshade when it's hot, and it makes a good umbrella when it rains or sleets or snows. He also uses his hat to carry water to his horse from a creek or water hole.

Getting his hands wet must have started a tickling in Dragonfly's nose, because right away he let out another long-tailed sneeze. This time the tail was a trembling neigh, sounding like a worried horse crying across the woods to another horse.

Ever since Dragonfly had found out he was going to get to go to the Rockies for the hay fever season and his mother had bought him that fine Stetson, he'd been strutting around in his also-new, high-heeled, pointy-toed cowboy boots. Watching him that week, anybody could have seen that cowboy boots were meant for show-off and for riding more than for comfort. They certainly weren't meant for running, and they weren't easy to walk in.

Imagine an ordinary man or boy wearing high-heeled shoes! Of course, a rider has to have high-heeled, pointed-toed shoes. They fit better in the stirrups, and the high heels keep his feet from going on through. What if a rider should accidentally get thrown off his horse when one foot was clear through the stirrup? He'd be dragged head down and maybe lose his life.

But it wasn't any use to stay mad at Dragonfly. It seemed a waste of bad temper I might need some other time. His imaginary horse couldn't drink much water anyway. So I killed the old cat's ninth life, swung out of the swing, and crossed the road to where he was still talking to my horse, Silver.

Pretty soon Dragonfly and I were on the way to the gang meeting.

We stopped for a few minutes at the bottom of Bumblebee Hill where the Little Jim Tree grows. "Here," I said to him, "is where Little Jim killed the bear."

"Whoa, Silver! Whoa! You big restless critter, you! Stand still!"

I could see Dragonfly was having a lot of fun pretending he was the famous masked marshal of the Old West. Because, as I've already told you, it would have been a waste of bad temper for me to stay really angry with him, I made a dive for his horse's bridle, went through an acrobatic struggle to stop him from rearing and plunging, and quickly tied his reins to the trunk of the Little Jim Tree.

But in my mind's eye I was seeing again the fierce old mother bear that had been killed here when Little Jim had accidentally rammed the muzzle of Big Jim's rifle down her throat and pulled the trigger. He had saved his own life and maybe the rest of our lives also. That was why we'd named the tree the Little Jim Tree.

Because it was getting close to the time we were supposed to meet the gang at the Snatzerpazooka Tree down by the swimming hole, I got a bright idea. I quickly rolled to my feet from where I'd been lying in the grass, made a dive for Silver's reins, untied them from the tree, and sprang into the saddle.

With a "Hi-yo, Silver!" I started off on a wild gallop for the bayou rail fence, with Dragonfly racing along behind me and yelling, "Come back here with my horse! After him, Tonto! Shoot him down!"

Tonto shot a few times with Dragonfly's saucy voice making him do it, but I knew Tonto and I were supposed to be good friends, so I didn't let any of his imaginary bullets hit me and tumble me off my big white stallion.

It took us only a little while to get to the river birch, where the scarecrow was still hanging, swinging in the breeze and looking like a bedraggled skeleton wearing dirty, faded, ragged clothes. His matted floor-mop hair still covered his face, and he looked pretty fierce.

We'd been panting there only a few minutes, resting on the long, mashed-down bluegrass, before I heard flying footsteps coming up the path from the spring. It was Poetry first, the barrel-shaped member of the gang. Right behind him were Circus, our acrobat, and Little Jim himself with his mouselike face and his tattered straw hat. The second Little Jim got there, I noticed that he had beads of perspiration standing out all over his forehead.

He stopped, looked down at us, grinned, and reached his forefinger to his forehead. Leaning over at the same time, he wiped off all the drops of sweat. The wind blew some of the salty drops onto my face.

Soon Big Jim, carrying a flashlight and a roll of burlap gunnysacks, came swinging along from the direction of the bayou, and we were ready for our important meeting. It was important because—well, because. I'll tell you why in just a minute.

Big Jim had an air of mystery about him. The jaw muscles below his earlobes were working the way they always do when he is thinking hard about something important. I wished he'd hurry up and start the meeting.

We were lying in the grass in several different directions and also tumbling around—all except Dragonfly, who was trying to hang his still-wet hat on the cross arm of the scarecrow so that it could dry.

Dragonfly was disgruntled about something. I could tell by the expression on his face. I found out why when he mumbled, "Whoever said to water your horse by letting him drink out of your cowboy hat ought to be horse-whipped." Then he plopped himself down on the ground, winced, and took off both new high-heeled cowboy boots.

"Too hot to wear high boots?" I asked, admiring the very pretty leather. I still wished I had a pair, but I was glad I could feel the fresh air on my already too-hot bare feet.

He shook his head no but sighed the way my dad does when he takes *his* shoes off after or before supper to rest his feet.

"Feet hurt?" I sort of whispered to Dragonfly, hoping they did but trying not to be angry at him anymore.

It was when I saw the small blister on his right heel that my temper fire almost went out. Whenever I see anybody in pain, it always hurts my heart and makes me want to stop the pain if I can. Someday, maybe, I'll be a doctor. I was thinking that when Big Jim called the meeting to order.

As soon as we were as quiet as we usually are at a gang meeting, Big Jim said to us grimly, "You guys get set for a lot of hard work. We have to do something not a one of us'll want to do."

"What?" a chorus of voices asked him.

And he answered, "We have to go up into the hills and dig up a dead dog and bury it over again."

"*Why?*" I asked, knowing what dog he meant. It was my cousin Wally's dog, Alexander the Coppersmith, who had gotten killed in a wildcat fight.

"Because," Big Jim said, "I just met Old Man Paddler down at the mouth of the cave, and he said so. He said the very first time there's a flash flood up there in the hills, that canyon will have a rush of water and Alexander'll get washed out and carried down the canyon to the creek. He would like us to dig him up and bury him in Old Tom the Trapper's dog cemetery. Do you think your cousin Wally would care if we moved Alexander's remains to a better place and gave him a more honorable burial?" Big Jim asked.

"I don't know. Maybe not. But he kind of wanted him to stay there right where he fell in battle," I answered.

"How're you going to carry a dug-up dog?" Little Jim asked.

"In one of these." Big Jim showed us the roll of burlap bags he had brought.

We all had sober faces, remembering how Little Jim could easily have lost his life when the wildcat had made a savage, spread-clawed leap toward him, away up there on a ledge of the canyon wall. Little Jim was saved only because Wally's dog had met the wildcat in midair before he could reach Little Jim.

"I move we do it," Little Jim said, and in a few seconds we had all voted yes.

"We'll use Old Man Paddler's spade and shovel," Big Jim announced.

The meeting was soon over, and we were on our way to exhume the body of one of the finest dogs there ever was, in order to bury it in a better place. We didn't have any idea that we would also revive an old mystery that had almost been forgotten around Sugar Creek.

2

We were untangling ourselves from our lying down positions and getting ready to start toward the old sycamore tree and the cave. We would go through it to the basement of Old Man Paddler's cabin—to get his spade and shovel, to go still farther up into the hills, to dig up the body of Alexander the Coppersmith, to take it to the haunted house, and to bury it under the big sugar maple tree in the fenced place we all knew as Old Tom the Trapper's dog cemetery. While we were getting ready to start to do all that, something happened.

It wasn't very important, and it only took a few seconds for it, but it shows you what kind of weather it really was that day. And the weather had a lot to do with the most important part of our sensational adventure.

As I've already told you, it was the kind of day when every now and then a whirlwind would come along out of almost nowhere. Then, after a few minutes of swirling leaves and dust, it'd be gone, and nature would settle down again to a stifling hot day.

Well, suddenly, while Dragonfly's new Stetson cowboy hat was drying on the left shoulder of the scarecrow swinging from the overhanging branch of the Snatzerpazooka Tree, there came spinning toward us from the direction of the bayou one of the biggest whirlwinds I'd ever seen. At the top of its cone, which reached high into the sky, were more dust and dry leaves and what looked like feathers and other things than you could shake a stick at.

The cornfield it was driving across was making a lot of noise. Its thousands of blades were tossing like a green lake in a windstorm. It was such a pretty sight it almost hurt my heart to see it. Nature around Sugar Creek can make a boy feel like that maybe a dozen times a day.

In almost nothing flat, the whirlwind was where we were. It whammed into the Snatzerpazooka Tree, shaking its branches and whipping Snatzerpazooka into an excited jiggling. Before you could have said, "Jack Robinson Crusoe," Dragonfly's drying Stetson was off the cross arm and gone.

I saw it leave the shoulder of the scarecrow even while I was holding onto my own straw hat to keep it from blowing off. I caught a glimpse of it sailing like a flying saucer out across the sky toward the creek, saw it land in the water, and saw also the ordinarily quiet face of Sugar Creek churning and tossing as the whirlwind went storming on over it to the other side.

No sooner was Dragonfly's hat off and on its way toward the creek than our spindle-legged little sneezer was on his way after it. In another couple of seconds, he'd land in the water himself with a splash.

"Hey!" I yelled after him. "Watch where you're going!"

But he didn't. He kept on like a baseball fielder after a high fly, running backward and sideways and forward.

It was all over in a few seconds. He was in and down and under and up, sputtering and spitting water, while the rest of us howled at how funny it was. The hot-tempered, extra-large whirlwind was already busy stirring up new excitement among the willows on the other side of the creek.

Well, the way that worked-up little guy stormed out into the excited water, grabbed up his Stetson, and started back as wet as a drowned rat and sneezing was almost funnier than when he had first landed in the water.

That showed what kind of weather it was and also how much Dragonfly thought of his new hat. He was so proud of it. I couldn't blame him in a way, because it was a very pretty hat. And in spite of its making his small face look still smaller, it did make him look like a Westerner—or, as Dad said when he saw it, "like an Easterner gone Western."

Dragonfly had his hat, but he looked worried when he came splashing back to where we were. Not a one of us needed to ask him why, because we knew.

I guess we all had mothers that worried about their sons and couldn't help it, since that is the way mothers are made. But Dragonfly had been having a hard time growing up because his very nice mother worried *too much* about him, or so it seemed to us.

Sometimes when he would even accidentally do some foolhardy thing such as he'd just done, he'd get a licking with his mother's sharp tongue. And yet, as my own mother once said, "Mrs. Gilbert is one of the finest mothers in the whole Sugar Creek territory. She's just impulsive. She's always sorry afterward when she has punished him unjustly. She's such a likeable person most of the time."

And then my kind of wonderful mother said something that was good for even a boy to know: "We mothers have to learn that we're supposed to mother our sons, not smother them with too much supervision."

I wasn't sure what she meant, but it sounded as if she liked Dragonfly's nervous mother in spite of the many mistakes she made because of her nerves.

Dragonfly was shivering now, standing under the Snatzerpazooka Tree, holding his wet hat, sniffling a little, too, and trying to get over his temper. All the angry feeling I'd had toward him for being so uppity about his fancy hat and cowboy boots was washed away.

He picked up his boots and with a sob in his voice said, "What'll I do! My mother will—" He stopped. I could see he liked his worrywart mother a lot and didn't want to say anything unkind about her. He finished what he had started to say, but I could tell it wasn't really what he'd started to say. "My mother will feel bad. She used her egg money to get me these new jeans."

Without thinking, I spoke up. "You're about my size. You can wear one of my shirts and a pair of my jeans till yours dry. It'll only take a jiffy to get them. Come on, everybody! Follow me!" And I was off on the run toward our house.

It didn't take long to get there because I was riding Silver at the time—not letting anybody know it—and the gang behind me was a mob of rustlers on ordinary horses trying to catch up with me to hang me from the nearest tree.

I left the gang at the walnut tree swing, where Poetry and Circus started waking up one of my old dead cat's nine lives. They were standing up right away, facing each other, and pumping hard to swing high.

Quickly I went into the house, through the kitchen, and into the back bedroom to the wardrobe. I was reaching for a shirt and a pair of jeans from the carefully ironed, folded, and mended supply that Mom kept there on a shelf, when I heard a woman's step and a rustling dress behind me.

Right away Mom started asking questions about why and what for and for whom. I guess it must have seemed odd to her that a son who already had on all the clothes a boy could stand on such a sultry day should want another shirt and another pair of jeans.

There were so many questions so fast that,

spying a palm-leaf fan on the dresser, I picked it up and started fanning myself and sighing and saying, "Excuse me, I feel smothered. Mothers are supposed to mother their sons, not smother them."

I got as mischievous a grin on my face as I could to show her I wasn't giving her a calling down, which a boy should never do to his mother for two reasons. The first reason is that a boy's father nearly always finds out and pretty soon smothers the boy with a beech switch. The second reason is that there is a verse in the Bible that says, "Honor your father and your mother," and nobody can honor his mother by being smart-alecky with her.

Anyway, as soon as Mom found out why and what for and for whom and how long, she picked out a pair of jeans and a shirt as nearly like the ones Dragonfly had on as she could find. Since he was only a little smaller than I was, the clothes fit pretty well.

"Don't you worry one little bit," Mom crooned to Dragonfly, who in spite of the hot day was shivering from being so wet. "With this sunshine and wind, your clothes will be dry in a little while. I'll have them ironed and ready for you by the time you get back."

We had to tell her what we were going to do up in the hills and at the haunted house, because I was her boy, and she could always work or rest better if she knew where I was and why.

Dragonfly went into our toolshed to change

clothes, and, while we waited, Mom got an idea. "If you're going to stop at Mr. Paddler's cabin, take these cookies along. *All the way*," she added with a smile at the gang and an unnecessary look at her only son. "I just baked them yesterday, so they're nice and fresh."

I stared at the frosted cookies, surprised that Mom had baked them yesterday and I hadn't found out about it until right now. Maybe that's why there were so many of them left.

A few seconds later, when Dragonfly came out of the toolshed with a grin on his face, it was as if I was facing a full-length mirror and walking slowly toward myself—except that I had on a broad-brimmed Stetson, was wearing a different face and a pair of fancy, high-heeled cowboy boots, and was carrying a coil of rope. I was also limping a little.

The rope was one I myself had bought out of my allowance a few days before. I had been practicing lassoing different things around the farm.

Dragonfly let out a whoop, swung the rope in a wide circle, and let it fly through the air with the greatest of ease. Its noose settled around the iron pitcher pump. He seemed to want to take the rope along with us, so—since I was trying to get all the way over being jealous of him because of his boots and Stetson—I let him.

I noticed the little guy wince when he limped over to slip the noose off the pump. I remembered the blister on his heel and asked him, "Feet hurt? Your boots too tight, maybe?"

He right away stopped limping and shook his head as much as to say that, even if his foot did hurt, it didn't hurt enough to admit it—not when he was so proud of his new, high-heeled, tooled-leather boots.

I liked the little guy for being brave, but I was remembering one of Dad's favorite quotes, "It's better to have good sense than it is to be brave."

If Dragonfly didn't have good sense for himself, somebody ought to have it for him, I thought. And that's why, just before we left, I went into the house to the drawer where we kept our first-aid kit and took out a small roll of gauze, some tape, and a few Band-Aids. I shoved them into one of my overall pockets. If I couldn't talk any good sense into Dragonfly's stubborn head, maybe the too-tight leather boot could—especially since it would be hard walking in the hills and it was quite a long distance to the haunted house.

Finally we started. It was a nice day even though it was still very sultry. I couldn't help but notice there were a few extralarge white clouds like mountain-sized piles of cotton in the southwest sky above the hills in the direction we were going.

"Look at those thunderheads!" I said to the rest of us. "We'd better get Alexander the Coppersmith dug up and moved. There might be a flash flood even this afternoon!"

"Good idea," Big Jim answered, and we all broke into a run—even Dragonfly, who had to in order to keep up.

It would save us almost a mile to go through the cave to Old Man Paddler's cabin instead of taking the long way around through the woods by the wagon trail. In a little while we were at the hollow sycamore in which I had gotten stuck one time. You've probably read about that in the story *Western Adventure*. I'd had to stay until way into the night and got scared half to death. Talk about a hair-raising experience! But that's another story. I have to stay with this one now.

Soon we were in the cave, working our way along in the light of Big Jim's flashlight, following the narrow passageway, stooping here, turning right or left here or there, getting a little higher all the time, until pretty soon we were at the wooden door that opens into the old man's cellar. He had left it unlocked for us.

The first thing I noticed when we were up the cellar steps and into his kitchen, which was also his living room, was the big map of the world mounted on the wall above his wooden dining table. Sticking in the map in different places were a lot of colored pins—some in Africa, some in India and China and in different other countries.

Just in case you've never been in Old Man Paddler's cabin, I'd better explain that he called the map his "prayer map." I'd been in his house quite a few times when he had other company, and he would always tell whoever was there, "It helps me remember to pray for my missionary friends. These different-colored pins show me just where they are and with what mission board. I can send up a prayer for them at any time."

The teakettle was singing on the stove, and in an open kettle beside it were chips of sassafras roots boiling. Sassafras tea was what he always made for us when we visited him.

The tea wasn't quite ready, so we looked around to see if there were any chores we could do for him, such as carrying in more firewood, sweeping the pine needles from his porch, or carrying a pail of fresh water from his spring. Little Jim, who, as you maybe know, was more interested in music than any of the rest of us, asked if we could play the old man's musical photograph album.

Old Man Paddler had quite a few of what Mom called antiques, such as a little hand sewing machine, an inkstand with two crystal ink bottles with caps, and a pen rack formed by deer antlers. In the loft upstairs was a hardwood swing cradle with casters so it could be rolled away, and it had very fancy ornamental carving on it. The cradle didn't tip or roll, and when you made it swing, it didn't make any noise.

But the antique we all liked best was the musical photograph album. It was worth going all the way up to his cabin just to see it and listen to it.

"Surely you can," the old man answered Little Jim. "You know where it is."

I followed Little Jim around behind the

stairway and stood beside him, while I watched him get it. I was thinking that long, long, long ago must have been a very interesting time to live. The album was about a foot long and maybe nine or ten inches wide and five inches high.

Old Mr. Paddler called to us then, saying, "Bring it in here, will you? I want to tell you something special about it, now that you're going to play it."

We carried it carefully and set it on the kitchen table. In the light from the window it was certainly pretty. Its front had artificial flowers on what looked like transparent celluloid. There were red roses in the middle and violets on the side all around. It was also bordered with gold. The album part had a lot of storage places the old man called "cabinets," and in them were pictures of Sarah Paddler, his wife, now in heaven, and his two boys, also in heaven, whose bodies are buried in the cemetery on Bumblebee Hill. There were also pictures of other people who used to live a long time ago around Sugar Creek.

"Here, boys, is what I want you to see." He turned the pages of the album with his gnarled old fingers until he came to the picture of a man with a long beard, hair that reached to his shoulders, and sad—very sad—eyes. "This, boys, is Old Tom the Trapper."

We were in a little huddle around the table, all of us looking at the tintype of Tom the Trapper, which, of course we'd all seen before maybe a hundred times. My own thoughts were kind of sad as I was reminded of what we'd come to do—exhume the body of Alexander the Coppersmith and rebury it under the big sugar maple tree near the house where Old Tom used to live. It was also where the old trapper himself was buried.

Maybe a hundred times, as I said, we had visited Old Man Paddler, and almost that many times he had told us Old Tom's sad story—how he'd been shot by an Indian arrow. We had acted out the story in a make-believe game many a time.

I always got to play Old Tom and get shot. Then, because I was too heavy to be carried, I would walk all the way to the haunted house with the gang, stretch myself out on the ground under the big tree, and they'd pretend to bury me—sometimes covering me over with autumn leaves and sometimes actually sprinkling dirt in my face, which would always break up the funeral.

"Old Tom used to have an album exactly like this," Old Man Paddler said. He stopped to turn to his stove and take off the kettle of sassafras roots, which were boiling too hard and might boil over.

"My twin brother, Kenneth, and I liked it so well that we used to go over to see him and ask him to let us play it. One Christmas we found a big brown package on our doorstep, and there it was. We thought at first he had given us his, but he hadn't. He'd bought us one just like it.

"Tom would be pleased if he knew what you boys are going to do today," the quavering voice of the old man went on as he poured our six cups of red sassafras tea. "He was a great lover of dogs."

It seemed nice to sit there in the friendly cabin and dream of the long-ago days, though we knew we'd better hurry to get done what we had to do. The musical album had a Swiss music box in it, and the music certainly was sweet. It could play three different tunes. Anybody who has ever heard a Swiss music box knows what they sound like. The air I liked best was the one we all knew by the name of "Silent Night," which nearly everybody in the world knows. It was playing right that second while we finished our tea.

Old Tom's story was different from any we'd ever heard. He wasn't the only living thing the Indians killed that long-ago year. Tom had wakened one morning to start on his trapline and had found both his Dalmatian dogs lying dead, killed by War Face's arrows.

"Terry and Jerry were the most beautiful dogs my brother and I ever saw," we'd heard Old Man Paddler say many times. I could repeat almost word for word that part of the story.

"Old Tom never married and for a long time hadn't had a living relative, so he kept himself from getting lonesome by always having a dog or two around the place.

"The two dogs I remember best were his Dalmatian twins, Jerry and Terry. It was a happy sight to see him strolling through the woods, playing his mouth organ and with those frisky, happy dogs galloping all around him, running on ahead, stopping to look back and up at him to see where he was going or if he was following.

"Old Tom was never quite the same after they were killed. He buried them close to the house under the sugar maple tree and put up twin markers for them. I think maybe that's why, when Kenneth and I found him with the arrow in his chest and he knew he was mortally wounded, his dying request was that he be buried under the big tree, too."

Old Tom had died before he could finish what he wanted to say. But the Paddler twins had heard his last few gasping words. "You boys—don't forget to serve God all your lives."

There were a few other words, which they couldn't hear, but they heard the word "saved" and something about music.

"I think Tom was trying to quote a Bible verse," Old Man Paddler told us. He quoted for us the verse he thought it was: "Believe in the Lord Jesus, and you will be saved."

I'd learned that verse in the Sugar Creek Sunday school when I was little. It seemed a whole lot more important now that we knew it was the last thing Old Tom the Trapper had thought just before he died.

As soon as we finished our sassafras tea and a frosted cookie apiece, the kind old man yawned and said, "You'll find my spade and shovel out in the toolshed. If I'm asleep when you bring them back, just clean them good and stand them behind the apple barrel. Help yourself to an apple apiece while you're there—before you go, I mean, and after you get back too." His voice was half-smothered in a sleepy yawn.

Little Jim piped up then. "What became of Old Tom's album when he died?"

For a minute Old Man Paddler got a far-away look in his eyes as if he was remembering something or else had just forgotten something. Then he said, "It was never found. His house had been broken into that same day and a lot of provisions taken. Kenneth and I always supposed maybe War Face or some of his renegade Indians took it. The kind old trapper died intestate too and—"

"What's that? What's intestate?" Little Jim cut in to ask.

I'd never heard the word before myself. The answer surprised me.

"It means he died without making a will saying who should get his things. They never found one, anyway." Old Man Paddler yawned again kind of noisily, which was the same as saying we could hurry along now if we wanted to, because he wanted to take his afternoon nap.

We soon had the spade and shovel and our apple apiece and were on our way. We were as far as the spring where the old man gets his drinking water when he called to us.

His high-pitched, quavering voice stopped us all in our tracks. "You know the spot where

Tom's grave is, boys, and Terry and Jerry are in the southeast corner of the little enclosure—just in case you may have forgotten. You might want to put Alexander in the southwest corner under the elderberry bush!"

He was standing in the doorway of his cabin, holding open the screen. I guess I never did see him standing like that without thinking how much he looked like one of the pictures of Moses I have in my *Child's Story Bible*. His hair was as white as snow, and his long flowing beard covered his chin and chest all the way to his belt.

We thanked him, told him we'd do what he suggested, and again were on our way, hurrying along because it had begun to look more like rain.

We tried to act happier than we were and laughed and joked a little, but all the time I was thinking how my cousin Wally's city-bred dog had given his life to save Little Jim.

That set my mind to daydreaming again. In my imagination I was up in the hills watching the fierce mother wildcat make a savage-tempered, spread-clawed leap for Little Jim's throat. Then I saw Alexander the Coppersmith meet her in midair, head and teeth first. I watched their fierce fight there on the high ledge. Finally both the wildcat and Alexander fell over the edge of the cliff to the rocks below.

And suddenly I was back in history more than nineteen hundred years, looking up at three crosses on a hill. And the Person on the middle cross was the Savior, dying for the sins of all the people of all the world, to save everybody who wants to be free from sin.

My thoughts were interrupted right then by Poetry. He and I were behind the rest of the gang. "*Psst!* Bill! Stop a minute. I want to show you something!" His tone of voice had an exclamation point in it that seemed to say, as it often does when he stops me like that, "I've just thought of something very important!"

"What?" I answered, stopping and standing stock-still.

"Remember what Old Man Paddler said? How we ought to clean his tools good before we put them away?"

"Sure," I answered. "What of it?" My father had taught me to do that, too. We never put away a spade or a shovel or a hoe or any other farm tool without first being sure it was clean.

"Just this," he said. "See this shovel? The last person who used it put it away without cleaning it."

I was studying the dirty shovel and was about to say, "Maybe the old man forgot," when Poetry suggested, "Wasn't the toolshed door unlocked? Couldn't anybody have sneaked in day or night, borrowed a shovel, and used it and put it back without the old man hearing him? He's hard of hearing, anyway."

"Sure," I said, "but—"

"And couldn't whoever used it have been digging somewhere, burying treasure or stolen money or something?"

Now he was getting, or trying to get, a mystery started in my mind. He had a mind like a detective's anyway. But this wasn't any time to be thinking things like that. We had to dig up a dog's body from a canyon floor and bury it in a dog cemetery under the sugar maple tree near the haunted house.

"Furthermore," Poetry said, with a frown on his forehead, "this yellowish clay on the shovel is not the kind of soil in Old Man Paddler's garden. His is *black*."

He was right, of course, but so what? "He could have been digging sassafras roots with it down along the creek or near the swamp."

Poetry scoffed at the idea. "This clay is the kind that is deep—way down deep. Why would he want to dig so deep? And why would a man who can't stand to put his tools away without cleaning them not clean his shovel?"

"Because maybe he's getting old and forgetful," I suggested.

But Poetry rejected my idea and held onto his.

3

All the rest of the way to Alexander the Coppersmith's grave in the canyon, I kept thinking about what Poetry had called to my attention. It wasn't very likely Old Man Paddler had put away his shovel without first cleaning it. And it did seem strange that the dirt on it was a yellowish clay, not the kind of soil in the old man's garden. Not unless he had been digging a lot deeper than would be necessary.

Well, coming to Alexander's grave was almost as sad a time as a funeral in the Sugar Creek Church. After about a fifteen-minute hike, we came to the place where the big old ponderosa had been blown over in a storm and formed a natural bridge across the canyon.

For a few seconds I was remembering that fierce fight Alexander had had with the wildcat on the ledge on the other side. Then I looked down to the bottom of the canyon to where the fight had ended, where Wally's mongrel and the killer wildcat had landed with the dog's teeth sunk into the wildcat's throat, and where they both had died.

Close to where they had landed, I saw now a little pile of stones, which is all the grave marker there was for a dog hero that had been one of the finest, even if the one of most un-controllable, quadrupeds there ever was.

For a second I felt hot tears stinging my eyes as I recalled some of the wonderful experiences we'd had with Alexander. It hurt my heart that never again would that beautiful copper-colored dog live and move and have his being—not at Sugar Creek or at his home in Memory City, Indiana, or anywhere. All that was left of him was lying down there under a pile of stones.

Near the pile of stones, a small stream trickled down the canyon, and I realized that Old Man Paddler was right. A flash flood would fill that narrow gulch with roaring water that would wash those stones away as though they were chips from a woodpile.

I looked toward the sky and noticed how blue it was except in a few places. In one place in particular there was a heavy buildup of sky-high, yellowish white clouds.

Each of us was thinking his own thoughts, and I supposed maybe they were more or less alike until Dragonfly all of a sudden spoke up in his worried voice, asking, "Where does a dog's soul go after it dies? Is there such a thing as a dog's ghost?"

Poetry scoffed at the idea of a dog having a ghost. "Of course not! Whoever heard of such a thing?"

"My mother," Dragonfly answered. "She heard a strange dog's voice howling in the direction of the swamp last night. It might have been Alexander the Coppersmith's! Hey! Listen! Hear that! There it is now!"

There was a ghostlike quaver in *his* scared voice. A second later when I did hear a faint bark or bawl or howl of a dog far away in the hills somewhere, it sent a shower of shivers up and down my spine. Right away there was another long howl, a little louder. For some reason it did sound almost exactly like the dog voice of Alexander the Coppersmith.

We were all so quiet for a few tense seconds that you could have heard a hummingbird's buzzing wings.

Then Big Jim said gruffly, "Imagination! Let's get going!" He led the way toward the rim of the canyon.

Dragonfly held back. There was a pained expression on his face, and I remembered the blister on his heel.

Even Little Jim hesitated. I saw his lip quiver, and, being close to him at the time, I heard him say under his breath, "He died to save me." It was a little like being in church. The words made me remember a sermon I'd heard once about Jesus dying on the cross.

"All right, boys—Bill, Poetry, Circus! We'll go down and get him. Dragonfly, you and Little Jim wait here. We'll be right back."

In a little while, the four of us older, bigger boys—I was the littlest of the four, the most slender, anyway—had the exhuming done, the corpse in one of the burlap bags, and a stretcher made out of the other one. And then the six of us were on our way to the haunted house and the little enclosure under the sugar maple tree where Old Tom the Trapper and his twin Dalmatian dogs were buried.

I noticed as we ambled along, the four of us bigger boys acting as pallbearers, that Dragonfly was limping quite a bit now. Maybe that was one of the reasons Big Jim hadn't asked him to help carry the dog. Little Jim was carrying the spade and Dragonfly the shovel.

After a while, though, when Little Jim begged to be a pallbearer, I carried the spade, and Dragonfly and I followed along behind. "Your foot hurt pretty bad?" I asked him.

That little guy must have hated to admit that such pretty cowboy boots could give him a sore foot. He winced, stopped, stopped limping, and skipped a little as if to say, "Certainly not," and kept on walking.

"Listen," I said to him. "You've got to be sensible. Here. The gang doesn't need to know it." I pulled him aside behind a little clump of blue spruce, leaned the spade against one of them, and taking out of my pocket a couple of Band-Aids, ordered him, "All right, sonny, let's have a look."

It helped me feel important to make Dragonfly take off his fancy right boot and let me put a Band-Aid on the raw place on his heel. It felt even better to hear him say a little later as we were walking along and he wasn't limping even a little, "Maybe I'm your almost-best friend."

Then Dragonfly took a deep breath, sneezed a long, friendly, neighing sneeze, let out a "Hi-yo, Silver!" and started off on the gallop to catch up with the others.

That's your reward, doctor! I said to myself. *And you can't charge him, because you got more out of it than he did.*

Pretty soon we were at the haunted house, not far from where I myself had lain at least half a dozen times just before the gang had buried me with leaves or sprinkled dirt in my face.

"Look what last week's windstorm did!" Dragonfly called out from where he was at the time, which was behind a small spirea shrub in full bloom.

Just mentioning last week's rain and windstorm carried my mind back to the fallen ponderosa bridge across the canyon. I took a look at what Dragonfly had called to us about. There, all twisted and bent out of shape, was the big H-shaped metal cap that I remembered had been on the top of the fireplace chimney.

My eyes flew to the roof of the old house. Sure enough, the brick chimney top up there was without its cap.

Little Jim piped up then and said, "That'll make it easier for Santa Claus to get in next Christmas."

I noticed he had a faraway expression in his eyes as if it were already December the twenty-fourth and time for eight imaginary reindeer to start drawing an imaginary old man in an imaginary sleigh from the North Pole to the rooftops of a hundred million houses all over the world.

"Let's get going," Big Jim ordered then.

He made a very dignified, sober-faced undertaker, saying to me, the grave digger, "Right over there, Bill. In the southwest corner under the elderberry bush where it looks like the gophers or moles have already started digging for us."

I looked under the elderberry bush, then stopped more stock-still than I had when Poetry had halted me a half hour ago. I just couldn't believe my eyes. Big Jim had said that gophers or moles had already started to dig there, and at first that was what it did look like. There was a little mound of yellowish clay to prove it.

Yellow clay! my astonished mind exclaimed. The same color of clay and the same type there had been—and still was a little of—on the shovel we had gotten from behind the apple barrel in Old Man Paddler's toolshed!

"What on earth!" I couldn't help exclaiming.

Poetry, who was standing and staring at what I was standing and staring at, let out an exclamatory whistle that also said, "What on earth!" or maybe, "What in the earth!"

From where Big Jim was, maybe it did look like the work of moles or gophers, but from where Poetry and I were—three feet from the little mound of earth—it was as plain as the crooked nose on Dragonfly's face that the pile of yellow clay could have been put there by a spade or a shovel.

It was a very fresh mound of earth, as if whoever had been digging and possibly burying something or somebody here had done it only yesterday or last night. Or even maybe that very morning.

Right that second the sun went under a cloud, and there was a rumble of thunder and a rustling of leaves in the trees as a noisy wind came sweeping through the woods. It was nature telling us that in a little while there would be an old-fashioned Sugar Creek thunderstorm.

While I was all mixed up in my mind as to who or what had been digging in Old Tom the Trapper's dog cemetery and who or what—if anything—had been buried there, and while the thought came that we would have to hurry and get Alexander buried again before the storm broke or we'd be like six drowned rats, Poetry cautioned me with his eyes and a shake of his head and with one forefinger to his lips.

I knew he was warning me not to tell the rest of the gang what he and I were suspicious of. We would not even mention the yellow clay on the shovel or the fact that the little mound of soil under the elderberry bush was the same kind of clay.

Just then it began to rain, the first drops large and scattered.

"Quick, everybody!" Big Jim ordered us. "Make a dive for shelter!"

We left our canine corpse in its gunnysack

44

coffin under the elderberry bush and shot like six two-legged arrows straight for the front door of the haunted house.

Big Jim had the key, having gotten it from Old Man Paddler, but it wouldn't unlock the rusty lock, and we couldn't wait long enough to keep on trying it, so we scurried around to the sloping cellar door, lifted it, and went down. Then we climbed the inside cellar steps, pushed up the trapdoor, and came out in the kitchen.

We hadn't any sooner let the trapdoor down again than the storm struck—really struck. The sky was like a big dome-shaped sieve with a million holes in it, and thunder and lightning broke loose as if they were trying to tear the world apart and scatter it all over everywhere.

As soon as our eyes got accustomed to the dimness, we walked around in the different rooms. Everything in the downstairs of the old house was the same as when we had visited it last. We stopped a while in the big living room, where the fireplace was, and talked about what an exciting time we'd had one snowy winter day when we'd been lost in a blizzard and had finally staggered into the house and started a fire here just in time to keep from freezing.

Little Jim, not knowing how serious Poetry's and my thoughts were, was in a playful mood. He made a beeline for the fireplace, stepped up on the long foot-high hearth, looked into the fireplace and up and exclaimed, "Boy! Is it ever big inside!"

Then he swung around and exclaimed to

us, "Here's where Santa Claus landed when he came down the chimney with a bound! Here, little round man," he called to Poetry, the roundest one of us, "come lay a finger aside your nose and give a nod and see if you can get back up again."

Poetry, not enjoying being reminded that he needed to go on a diet for a year, ignored Little Jim's joke and went instead to the window. There he looked out at Old Tom the Trapper's canine cemetery and at the muddy mound of dirt under the elderberry bush.

Not wanting Little Jim to feel squelched because nobody paid any attention to what he thought was a bright idea, I sat down on the fireplace hearth, stretched myself across it, looked in and up, and was surprised that I could see all the way to the top of the chimney. It certainly was big enough for a little round man to get down, even if he had a sack of toys on his back.

I ducked out again quickly. Since there was no cap on the top of the chimney and the damper was wide open, I'd gotten quite a few drops of rain in my face.

Poetry and I watched for a chance to get alone so that we could talk. Pretty soon we were by ourselves in the kitchen, standing on the trapdoor.

"Listen," he whispered. "Let's keep it a secret about the yellow clay for a while. We don't want to turn out to be a couple of chumps if that mound of dirt *was* made by a mole or a gopher. Or if maybe Old Man Paddler himself used the shovel somewhere and forgot to clean it."

We agreed and shook hands on it. Both of us felt better, although I kept wondering and also hoping our suspicions were right—especially when I remembered what I'd heard on the radio at home about somebody having escaped from prison and being armed and extremely dangerous.

Little Jim, who was still in a playful mood, all of a sudden came into the kitchen. "Let's play Goldilocks and the Three Bears!"

Well, there wasn't much of anything you could do, shut up in an empty house without any checkers or caroms or Ping-Pong to play. So to help ourselves pass the time while the storm was wearing off its temper outdoors, we took Little Jim up on his idea.

Big Jim started in by growling, "Somebody has been tasting my soup!"

Circus pretended to be the mother bear and complained about his soup having been tasted, too.

Then Little Jim piped up with tears in his mouselike voice, saying, "Somebody has been tasting my soup and has eaten it all up!"

Then we went into the living room, and Big Jim started growling about somebody having sat in his chair. A little later, we did what Goldilocks did—we went upstairs to the bedroom. And there we got the surprise of our lives.

There actually was a bed up there! It was not a bedstead with springs and mattress, but on the floor—near the window overlooking the creek—was a plastic air mattress with a built-in headrest. It was inflated and ready for anybody to sleep on. Folded at its foot was a blanket.

Little Jim didn't seem to realize that the mattress being there was anything unusual. Certainly he wouldn't think what Poetry and I were thinking! To him, this olive-colored air mattress was just something that made the game of Goldilocks and the Three Bears seem more real.

Quick as a flash he was across the room and stretched out full length on the mattress. His curly head was resting on the built-in pillow, and his high-pitched complaining voice was half sobbing, "Somebody has been sleeping in my bed—and here she is!" He didn't even wait for Big Jim or Circus to growl their complaints about somebody having slept in their beds first.

Now, I thought, Poetry and I had better tell the rest of the gang about our suspicions. I opened my mouth to say, "Somebody's using this old house for a hideout," but I got Poetry's right elbow in my ribs and a sharp shush in my ear. Then he whispered, "Let's wait till we dig under the elderberry bush and see what's buried there. Just as soon as it quits raining."

Big Jim was bothered, though, about the air mattress. All of a sudden he went to the closet we all knew about, unfastened the iron latch, and swung open the heavy oak door.

And there on a shelf was a row of canned goods and a two-burner camp stove. Also on the shelf was an aluminum cook kit with a plate, cup, frying pan, and a stewpan.

What on earth! Who was living in this old house and why?

Little Jim, still in his dreamy-eyed make-believe world, exclaimed, "Now we can start over again with somebody eating our real soup."

It was already beginning to get lighter outside, which meant that in a little while the rain would be over. We could go back downstairs and outdoors and hurry up and get Alexander the Coppersmith buried.

But behind me right then, Dragonfly whispered, "Gang! Come here! Look! Somebody's coming!"

In a scramble of six excited boys and twelve nervous feet, we rushed to the window and looked out. Running toward the house like a scared cottontail and carrying a rifle was a tall man in gray jeans. I could see he was bareheaded. His hair was mussed up, and he looked as if he needed a haircut almost as bad as a boy who hasn't had one for two months.

Boy oh boy oh boy! Talk about showers of shivers going up and down a boy's spine! When I saw that man carrying a rifle and hurrying through the rain toward the house, it was like a giant whirlwind coming into my mind. Who was the man? Where had he come from? Why was he running so fast? And why was he living here in this old house?

Was the man with the rifle the same person who had sneaked into Old Man Paddler's tool-shed, borrowed his shovel, dug with it in Old Tom the Trapper's canine cemetery, and buried something there? Or maybe dug up something? Was he the fugitive from justice the radio news-caster had been talking about so excitedly?

Another thought was tossed high in the whirlwind in my mind. Was there any kind of reward offered for the man, and if there was, would the gang be able to capture him and claim it?

It certainly seemed that long-legged rifle-man making a wet dash for the house we were upstairs in was bringing with him a lot of dan-ger. A whole lot of it!

"Looks like we're going to have company," Big Jim said as calmly as he could, maybe so as not to scare any of us any worse than we already were.

The window overlooking the creek also overlooked—right below us—the sloping out-side cellar door. And a minute later, I heard the cellar door open, heard steps hurrying up, heard the trapdoor squeaking on its hinges, and I knew that the man with the rifle was already in the kitchen.

Then he was in the living room. And then we heard his heavy steps on the stairs on his way up. Six boys were caught like rats in a trap.

"Quick!" Big Jim ordered. "Everybody in the closet!" He shoved us in ahead of him, and in seconds we were all inside and had the door shut.

"We're in a trap now!" Dragonfly whined in a scared whisper.

"*Sh!*" Big Jim cautioned us and none too soon, for I could hear the rifleman's heavy step at the head of the stairs. Any second now he would come down the long hall to the room we'd just left.

"We *are* in a trap!" Dragonfly persisted. "How can we get out?"

Again Big Jim shushed him. Then he whispered a command to all of us: "Follow me! But be quiet!"

His flashlight was focused on the row of wooden pegs on the side wall of the walk-in closet—pegs that we had decided the first time we were here had been used for coat hangers by Old Tom the Trapper years and years and years ago.

"Remember this?" Big Jim asked but didn't wait for us to answer. There wasn't time. His light was focused now on a small wooden peg on the wall by itself, just high enough for a little boy to use for his clothes.

And then I remembered.

Big Jim gave that low wooden peg a sideways yank. The whole back panel of the closet moved, and there in front of us was the dark attic where, on our first visit to the haunted house, we had seen the fiery eyes of a furry wild animal. But that's another story.

"Everybody in, quick!" Big Jim whispered his order.

As fast and as quietly as we could, we scrambled into the attic. I was glad the sound of rain on the roof was loud enough so that maybe the man now clomp-clomping toward the room we had just left couldn't hear us.

There was a bit more noise than there should have been on account of Dragonfly's high-heeled boots clattering on the board floor —but also for another reason. I actually had to force that little guy to go in ahead of me. He kept struggling and whispering in protest, trying to get back out into the closet. We didn't find out why until we were all inside and Big Jim had slid the panel back in place and we were standing in the black dark, trembling with excitement and hoping whoever was in the room where the air mattress was didn't know about the secret panel.

Almost the second the panel snapped shut, Dragonfly whined to us the reason he had been trying to get back out.

"My new hat!" he whispered. "It got bumped off! It's still in the closet! If he finds it, he'll know we're here and maybe shoot every one of us!"

4

Now what? It was still hard to keep my mind from acting like a whirlwind.

We were in a black attic in the upstairs of a haunted house. A fugitive with a rifle was also in the house and was already up the stairs. There wasn't any way we could get out except through the closet in the room where he was.

What if he found Dragonfly's hat? He'd know we'd been here—or *were* here—and what would he do to us? He had a rifle, and all we had was a rope, although we did have six times as many muscles as he had, and all of us had had experience using them in a life-or-death fight.

The rain on the roof made it seem safe for us to whisper, now that there were two doors separating us and the man. If he did hear anything, he might think it was only the storm outside. But how could we be sure one of the six of us wouldn't whisper too loud? One or the other of us might even forget and talk with his out-loud voice, and our hiding place would be found!

Also, one of us had a sensitive nose that was allergic to musty odors, dust, ragweed pollen, and almost everything else that wasn't fresh air. Any second while we were there in that dark attic, hardly daring to breathe, Dragonfly's nose might start to tickle, and he would have to sneeze.

The attic had a wild-animal odor as if there were mice around. It reminded me of the mother raccoon and her babies who had once lived here. The chimney at that time had had a big hole in its side, opening into the attic, and she'd used it as a secret door to her hideout.

Right then, while I was thinking about the musty odor in the attic, I could tell that Dragonfly's nose was smelling it. I heard him take in a trembling breath and knew he was trying hard not to do what I knew he was going to do. And then he did it.

Dragonfly sneezed!

There was sudden deathly silence in the attic and in the room on the other side of the closet. You could have heard a pin drop if it hadn't been for the rain on the roof. The next minute seemed like an hour while we waited to find out what, if anything, Dragonfly's smothered sneeze had done in the rifleman's mind.

Just then Little Jim whispered the craziest idea I'd ever heard. "That was a single-shot rifle, I could tell. Let's slide the panel open and go storming out and tackle him. He could shoot only one of us, and the rest of us could jump him and tie him up with our rope and—"

Big Jim's shush was almost louder than Little Jim's excited suggestion. One thing the little mouse-faced guy had said, though, gave me a spurt of hope. It reminded me that we did have a rope. It could come in handy if we had to get into a knock-down-drag-out fight with the fugitive. There might be a chance to use the rope as a lasso, the way cowboys of the Old West used to and the way today's cowboys do in roundups.

By this time I was accustomed to the sound of rain on the roof and could distinguish between it and the faint movements of the man on the other side of the closet. I tried to imagine what he was doing.

Of course, I couldn't see a thing—not until suddenly the closet door was yanked open and a shaft of light came through the crack in the sliding panel a few inches from the place where the small wooden peg was!

Since I was the closest to the crack, I could see the man peering in with his rifle ready to shoot. I really cringed then, thinking he had heard us and was coming in to get us.

His eyes flashed all around that closet from one corner to the other. I saw them focus on the shelf where the tinned goods and the camp stove were and heard him grunt, "Humph!"

He stooped a little so as not to bump his head and walked into the closet. But he stumbled over something on the floor and almost lost his balance. Then the man reached down to pick up what he had stumbled over, and it was Dragonfly's cowboy hat!

And that was enough to scare us all half to death, but at the moment I was the only one of the gang who knew what had happened.

I kept on watching. I saw the rifleman frown at Dragonfly's new, still-wet hat with its crushed crown and bent brim. I saw him take a quick look all around, then toss the hat out of the closet onto the air mattress. He was mumbling something under his breath.

And then, holding his rifle ready to shoot, he was moving cautiously back into and around the room as if he was expecting any minute to have to use the gun on somebody. He stood at the window, looking out toward the creek. *Who, I wondered, is he waiting for?*

He raised a raspy voice then and called in the direction of some other part of the upstairs, "Hey, you, Crimp! Where are you?"

I expected to hear another man's answering voice from somewhere in the house—maybe from the basement—even though *I* knew the crushed-crowned, twisted-brimmed Stetson belonged to Dragonfly Gilbert and not to anybody named "Crimp."

At the same time I seemed to remember a name I had heard in the newscast at our house, and it was Crimp the Shrimp!

At a time like that you don't do anything. You *can't* do anything except listen for all you're worth and wait. It was a good thing it hadn't been Dragonfly's eyes that had seen his beautiful, new, still-wet Stetson with its crushed crown and twisted brim, or he might have called out, "Stop! Leave that hat alone! That's my hat!" or something like that.

I think I'd never seen such a tired-faced

man—as well as grim-faced. He was yawning as though he hadn't had any sleep for two or three days and nights. I could see his face clearly now because he was standing again at the window that overlooked the creek.

Then he cocked his head to one side and listened. Two or three times he put his left hand up to his ear as though he was trying hard to hear any sound there might be.

He came and took another look into the closet, and I held my breath for fear he'd see through the crack I was looking through and see my eye. Again he turned his head sideways and listened in our direction with his left ear. Then I heard the heavy closet door squeaking on its rusty old hinges. A second later it went shut, and we were in the blackest dark I ever saw.

The second the door was shut, I heard the iron latch snap into place and also heard Dragonfly whisper, "We're locked in! We're in a trap for sure."

This time he was right. For sure.

Of course, I didn't tell him what I also knew —that his fancy Stetson was out in the bedroom with its crown crushed and its brim twisted. I only hoped the rifleman didn't try it on and find out it was too small for a man and couldn't possibly belong to Crimp the Shrimp.

We still hardly dared to breathe, and we almost were afraid to whisper. It was so quiet now on the other side of the closet that it was spooky.

Big Jim was the first to break our silence when he whispered, "Listen, everybody! Hear that?"

I listened as hard as I could, not knowing what to expect to hear but finding out a few seconds later.

Dragonfly let out a scared whisper. "There's a wild animal in here!"

But there wasn't. There wasn't a wild animal. It would have been funny if there had been, because any boy who has ever lived with a father has probably been awakened many a dark night by that same-sounding sound, like somebody using a handsaw on a board or a two-by-four or maybe a log.

Snzzzzzz—snzzzzzz—snzzzzzz—snzzzzzz!

Our rifleman had been so tired and sleepy he probably had lain down and gone to sleep.

He and Crimp had maybe escaped from jail together. They had broken into a store somewhere and stolen some canned food and a camp stove and had been hiding here. Maybe Crimp had stolen a new cowboy hat too, I thought. He had left the house a while—maybe to get more supplies. The rifleman had gone, too, and had just gotten back. Now he was so tired he just had to have some sleep.

But soon Crimp the Shrimp might come running in from somewhere, and we would have *two* dangerous men just outside our attic jail.

One thing we had to be thankful for was that Big Jim had his flashlight. We could see into every gable of the attic to satisfy our minds that there *weren't* any wild animals or ghosts. Our hardest part would be to keep still, to keep Dragonfly from sneezing, and to keep him from worrying about his hat out there in the closet, where I knew it wasn't.

We had to get out of that attic as quick as we could. We had to run like lightning to Poetry's house and phone the sheriff to tell him that two dangerous criminals were hiding in the haunted house. If only there had been a window in the attic, as there was in a lot of attics in the Sugar Creek territory, we could have opened it and climbed out.

Big Jim's flashlight right then was playing on the repaired place in the fireplace chimney, which used to be the mother raccoon's secret entrance into the attic from the roof of the house. As I remembered, she would climb the big sugar maple tree, crawl out on the over-hanging branch, drop down onto the roof, scamper up the chimney on the outside, and then scramble down the inside like a fur-coated Santa Claus, bringing food to her coon babies.

And then I almost gasped aloud at what I saw right then. Whoever had repaired the big hole hadn't done a very good job. The mortar they had used between the old bricks looked as if it hadn't been a good mixture. Some of it had crumbled out already and was on the attic floor. It was almost as fine as dust. I quickly scratched at some of the mortared places, and it was like sand. That's when I got what I thought was a bright idea.

"Listen," I whispered as quietly as I could, "all we have to do is scratch out this old sandy mortar to loosen the bricks and take out enough bricks to make a hole big enough for us to crawl through. We can tie our rope around the chimney right here, let ourselves down inside, and come out in the fireplace below. Then we can slip out through the basement and beat it for home."

Dragonfly *would* think of a reason why it wasn't a good idea. "What about my new hat? How would we get it out?"

We had to ignore his worry, though. My plan sounded good to Big Jim, so in a minute, at his orders, we had our knives out and were working away as quietly as we could, scratching out the poor mortar. In only a few minutes we had the first brick out.

Poetry, the roundest one of us, was a little worried. He was afraid our escape hole wouldn't be big enough for him. The chimney itself would be large enough, but maybe not the hole we were making.

Every few seconds we stopped to listen to see if we could hear our sleeping jailer snoring, and we still could. He *must* have been tired! Also, as everybody knows, rain on the roof makes anybody sleepy.

Brick number two came out in a little while, then number three. We were on number four when Big Jim's knife slipped out of his hand and fell, not on the outside but on the inside of the chimney and landed with a clatter on the floor of the fireplace below. The sound it made as it landed was enough to have wakened the giant in the story "Jack and the Beanstalk. "

There was a snort from the rifleman's nose like Dad's nose sometimes makes when he's been asleep and suddenly wakes up. It felt like ten whole minutes, although it was maybe only thirty seconds, before the rhythmic snoring was going on again and Big Jim had my knife and was digging away on another brick. In another few minutes, if all went well, we'd have a hole big enough for us to get through, and we'd soon be on our way out.

All went well until the last loose brick was removed, and then we discovered the opening was too small. It was big enough for Little Jim, Dragonfly, Circus, Big Jim, or me but hardly half large enough for Poetry.

It didn't feel very good having my plan squelched. It had seemed a wonderful idea—swinging ourselves down on a rope and coming out into the fireplace downstairs. While we'd been working to get out the bricks—even while I was scared that if the man heard, he'd come after us—I was also imagining what an exciting story it would be when I told my folks about it and that it was my very own idea.

The light that came down the chimney and into the attic took away the spooky feeling we'd had when we were in the very black dark, and we could see each other without the flashlight on.

The expression on Poetry's face as he studied the escape hole we had made was enough to hurt your heart. What he said right then showed what kind of boy he was, though, and how brave he was. "All right," he whispered. "You guys go ahead. I'll stay here and guard our prisoner!" Imagine pretending the rifleman out there was our prisoner!

Big Jim's face was grim as he decided for us what ought to be done. "We're not going off and leaving anybody here alone." Then he said, "If we don't hang together, we'll all hang separately!"

Besides, we'd probably make so much noise going down we'd be sure to wake the fugitive up, and then what would we do?

Little Jim came up with a bright idea—bright and also brave. "Let just one of us go. I'm the littlest. I could get down easier and quicker and could run to Poetry's house and phone the sheriff." Of course, we wouldn't think of letting that little guy do a thing like that.

"You couldn't lift the trapdoor by yourself," I discouraged him. "I could, but you couldn't."

Just saying that stirred up a whirlwind of shivers in my mind. What if *I* did it? And what if, while I was halfway down, somehow I got stuck in the chimney? Or what if the man heard me and came storming downstairs and caught me just as I landed in the fireplace?

Right in the middle of my mixed-up thoughts came another one. How on earth could a little round man, with a little round stomach that shook when he laughed like a bowlful of jelly, climb down and back out of a hundred million chimneys all in one night?

At that very second I got another idea. Maybe I could get *up* the chimney easier than down it and be outside the house quicker. I could scramble out onto the roof, swing myself up onto the overhanging branch, and work myself to the trunk of the tree and down without making much noise. Then I could run like a deer to Poetry's and phone the sheriff to say that a dangerous criminal had five boys locked in the attic of the haunted house.

I put my head through our just-made opening and looked up. I got a few rain splatters in my face. Then I looked down and saw how far it was to the fireplace below and got a cringing feeling. What would happen if, when I crawled into the chimney and started to go up and out, I should slip and fall and go down and out!

One thing I noticed, though. There was a brick jutting out about an inch from the chimney wall opposite the hole we had made. If we would put a board across to that little jutting, I could stand on it and as easy as pie go up and out and down.

I whispered my idea to the gang and was a little surprised that Big Jim took me up on it. He thought there ought to be two of us, though —Circus, our acrobat, and me. If one of us got stopped, the other one could go on anyway. It'd be like having a spare tire in a car trunk in case of a puncture or a blowout.

And so it was decided.

"I'll go first," I said.

But the whole idea wasn't any good unless we could find a loose board to use for a foundation for us to stand on. Where could you find a board in an attic unless you used one of the floorboards?

"There's bound to be a loose board here somewhere," Poetry whispered.

For a few stealthy minutes we followed Big Jim's flashlight beam all over the dusty attic floor, feeling our way on hands and knees to see if we could find a board that wasn't nailed down.

It was Dragonfly who found a loose board first. He hissed to us from the other side of the chimney, "Here's one!"

The board was not only loose, it also was the right width and length to use as a platform for me to stand on in the chimney. In a few seconds we had it up and out.

And six boys let out six startled gasps at what we saw under the loose board when we took it up. My thoughts were gasping louder in my mind than the six gasps made by six surprised boys had sounded in my ears. What I was looking down at in the light of Big Jim's flashlight was what at first just looked like an old flat box. But we brushed off the dust, and it was an album like the one we had just seen and heard in Old Man Paddler's cabin!

The red roses in the middle of the top weren't even faded. The violets around the outside edge were still blue, and the gold border still looked like gold. What on earth!

We had found Old Tom the Trapper's album!

What we had found seemed so important that for a few seconds we forgot about being locked in an attic by a vicious criminal and our plan for me to climb up and go flying to Poetry's house to phone the sheriff.

"Careful!" Big Jim cautioned when I started to open the album, but it was too late. I had accidentally released the spring of the music box. All of the sudden in that ghostly quiet we heard the very pretty strains of "Silent Night."

I guess I never heard sweeter music in my life, but that wasn't any time to enjoy it. Something else had been in the box too—a musty odor.

Dragonfly sneezed without having a chance to try not to, and the sneeze was a lot louder than is safe at a time like that.

5

Big Jim's always quick mind took charge of his muscles. In a flash he had the musical album back in its hiding place, and he was lying full length over where the board had been, completely covering it. Closing the album's beautiful flowered lid shut off the music, and in a second it was a silent day and all was calm —all, that is, except our nervous thoughts.

What, I worried, had the Christmas music and Dragonfly's sneeze done to the rifleman?

We listened in the direction of the air mattress and couldn't hear a thing except the sound of air blowing through a man's nose. He really must have been tired.

Sure now that our almost thundery noise hadn't wakened our jailer, we carefully stretched the board across the inside of the chimney, rested the other end on the jutting brick, and tested it to be sure it was going to be solid. It was.

Big Jim and Circus would hold the board in place by pushing hard on the attic end. The board was also long enough for somebody to sit on. In case the opposite end slipped off the brick, maybe they could hold me up the way one end of a teeter-totter holds up the other end when it has enough weight on it.

And now it was time to go. *Here, Bill Collins,* I gritted my teeth and said to myself, *here goes nothing!*

Into the chimney I went. First, I lay on my back on the board with my head in the opening and, with the gang helping a little, wormed my way until I was far enough in to sit up. The board under me made a good foundation for my weight. In a minute now, I'd be standing, looking out the top of the chimney. A minute after that I'd be out and onto the roof, and Circus would be on his way up after me.

It was hardly raining now. Even if it had been raining cats and dogs, it wouldn't have made any difference as far as my soot-covered clothes were concerned. They'd have to be washed anyway, and Mom always liked rainwater for washing.

It was easier than I had expected it would be. Now my head was out, my hands were on either side of the wide chimney top, and my feet were on my end of the teeter-totter. I braced myself to jump. I'd have to jump to get myself high enough to work the rest of myself the rest of the way up and out.

It was wonderful to breathe the fresh air after being in the musty attic. A robin on a branch of the maple tree was announcing that the storm was over. In the distance, lazy thunder was rolling, saying the same thing.

But there was another sound, and it wasn't being made by anything in nature. I looked in the direction it seemed the sound was coming from, which was toward the creek, and saw a boat with a man in it, rowing. In a few fleeting flashes, he would reach the shore on this side. I was so astonished that I almost forgot where I was.

It's Crimp the Shrimp! I thought.

The minute the prow of the oldish boat touched shore, the stranger, who seemed in a hurry, was on his feet and out of the boat. He gave it a shove, and it was out in the water and floating downstream. And then he was streaking like a deer for the cellar door of the house. Even as he ran, I saw him look up toward the roof.

I ducked to keep from being seen and whispered down to the gang, "There's somebody coming! He's running like a streak of lightning. He—"

That was as far as I got. All of the sudden I felt the bottom drop out. The board had slipped off the brick ledge, and I knew I was going down. I set my arm muscles to hold onto the chimney top with my hands. Maybe my feet could find the brick the board had been resting on.

But I didn't have a good grip on the extra-wide chimney. *Down and down and down and down!* I fell past the dark hole we had made, struggling to stop myself by grasping for the rough inside of the chimney, cringing and worrying and wondering what on earth and how soon and would it hurt and how much. I was on my way to the bottom of the soot-blackened, brick-lined chimney!

Well, it was not the night before Christmas, even though we'd had a little Christmas music. And there was a whole lot more than a mouse stirring. The rifleman who had settled his brains for a long afternoon nap would soon hear such a clatter he would wake up and spring from his air mattress to see what was the matter.

Also, out on the lawn making a beeline for the cellar door was an excited man in a hurry to get to the house and in it. And he and I would probably get to the fireplace at the same time.

"Down the chimney St. Nicholas came with a bound." That is the way a line in the poem goes.

I did manage to land on my feet, which meant that I didn't get hurt except for what felt like twenty scratches and bruises. But I certainly wasn't in any mood to "bound" or to call out "Merry Christmas" to anybody. Instead, there was a feeling in my mind that recalled to me the last words Santa Claus was supposed to have yelled after he got back up the chimney and was driving away. They were "Good night!"

Inside the fireplace, I heard the basement door opening and footsteps starting up to the closed trapdoor in the kitchen. I wished I could have been standing on that door and all the gang with me!

But in a minute the trapdoor would be open, the second man would be in the house, and, as Dragonfly had said quite a few times, I'd be in a trap.

My eyes glimpsed the big hall closet near the front door, and I wondered if I would have time to make a dive for it and get into it to hide.

Maybe, I thought, *Crimp the Shrimp will be in such a hurry to get upstairs that he'll swish past the fireplace without looking.* I knew the screen standing on the hearth certainly couldn't keep him from seeing me if he looked in my direction. I decided to risk the hall closet.

I shoved aside the fireplace screen and scrambled out. Then I stumbled over my own feet and managed a head-over-heels fall on the floor in front of the fireplace just in time for the man to trip over me.

I didn't have any idea how much soot there was in the chimney until I saw how much of it had brushed off on my clothes and hands and face onto the clothes and hands and face of the man I was in a tangled-up scramble with.

Before I could get up from the floor, I felt his arms around me, holding onto me like a boxer holding onto another boxer to keep from getting hit. Scared plenty, I was like a fishing worm trying to keep from being put on a hook, as I squirmed and twisted and panted and grunted and tried to use my fists.

But those arms around me were like the muscles of the village blacksmith under the spreading chestnut tree. They were as strong as iron bands. My own muscles weren't exactly weak, and my jaw muscles were extrastrong from eleven-almost-twelve years of exercise, and my teeth were good and sharp, which I proved to my assailant without knowing I was going to.

With a yank and a squirm and a couple of twists and a *wham-wham-wham* with my doubled-up fists, I was free all of a sudden and on my way toward the kitchen and the open trapdoor.

I wasn't quick enough, though.

Crimp the Shrimp or whoever he was got to the doorway first and blocked it. "You little brat!" he yelled at me. "Where'd you come from, anyway? How'd you get in here?"

I stood gasping, looking at his smudged face and hands and clothes, knowing how they had gotten that way. "I'm Santa Claus," I answered him, panting. "I just came down the chimney."

"Oh, you did, did you!" he said. "Well, you listen to me! You're old enough to know there ain't no Santa Claus, and in just about two seconds you'll find out for sure!"

With that, he made a lunge for me, and at the same time I let out a scream for help. Though, with the gang locked in the attic and the rifleman upstairs, how in the world could I expect any help?

"Help! Help! Big Jim! Circus! Everybody! *H—e—e—e—l—p!*"

While I was dodging this way and that like a mouse in a house with a woman with a broom after it, I glimpsed a movement in the fireplace, saw the end of a rope, and felt a spurt of hope. That rope meant Big Jim or Circus had tied one end of the rope around the chimney up there in the attic and had pushed the other end through our newly made hole and dropped it down for me to grab onto. I could pull myself up hand over hand to safety.

Except that it wouldn't *be* to safety. That would be going from a new trap back into an old one.

I couldn't get out the front door because it was locked. I couldn't get to the kitchen and the trapdoor because the way was blocked. The stairway was the only other way, and there was a man with a rifle up there.

That's when things really began to happen. I heard noisy action in the fireplace before I understood what was going on. And then it *was* like the night before Christmas, but instead of one little round man with a round stomach coming down, there swarmed down that rope three of the liveliest soot-covered Santa Clauses you ever saw or heard. Big Jim was first. He was out of the fireplace with a bound, followed by Circus and Little Jim.

Still, even though we all had muscles like the village blacksmith's, the man we were try-ing to capture was like a roaring lion. He had fists as hard as sledgehammers! I found that out when one of them landed *ker-whamety-squash* against my jaw, and I went down like a scarecrow cut loose from a tree branch.

I wasn't knocked out. I still had a few wits left, enough to see our cursing, grunting, fierce-fighting fugitive from justice roll out of

Big Jim's and Circus's and Little Jim's clutches. He shook them off like a bear shaking off a pack of dogs. Then I saw his right hand shove inside his jacket and whip out a pistol from a shoulder holster.

I was so close to being knocked out that I couldn't move, but I could yell, and I did. "Look out, everybody! He's got a gun! He's got a gun!"

"You bet I've got a gun, you little whipper-snappers! And I'm going to use it on the first little demon of you that makes another move!"

He was like a bear at bay as he stood crouching with his back to the fireplace. All of us stood in front of him. He was holding his pistol in one hand, and the doubled-up fist of the other hand was closed so tightly that the knuckles showed white. I knew that we had lost the battle and wondered what a man who was armed and extremely dangerous would do to a gang of boys?

That's when I saw the end of the rope in the fireplace behind him moving excitedly and heard a noise in the chimney. A second later a spindle-legged Santa Claus came down with a bound, stormed out of the fireplace, made a dive like a tackle stopping a quarterback, grabbed Crimp the Shrimp by one of his legs and held on for dear life, his face set like a bulldog's.

There was a crash as Crimp the Shrimp went down. He struck his head on a corner of the fireplace hearth, let out a groan, went limp, and lay sprawled on the floor.

Dragonfly, the poorest fighter of any of us and the most superstitious, was a hero. He had maybe saved one or more of our lives. All we would have to do now would be to get the rope out of the fireplace and tie up our prisoner. If there was a reward for capturing him, we could claim it.

In the back of my mind, though, was something else. There was more trouble upstairs. Where was the man with the rifle, the man who had been so dog tired he had lain down and gone to sleep and had slept all through our fierce, fast, fistfight with Crimp the Shrimp? What had happened to him?

We found out when we heard a step on the stairs. Looking up, we saw the man, the rifle in his hands, holding it ready to use if he thought he had to, or if he wanted to.

6

The rifleman had something else in his hands. To my astonishment, it was a pair of metal ringlike things with a chain connecting each to the other.

Handcuffs! my mind exclaimed. And my mind was right. What would he do with them? Which one of us would—

That was as far as I got to think, because right then Dragonfly cried, "Hear that! It's Alexander's ghost again! There's two of him now!"

I didn't even have to listen to hear. From outside the house there came a dog's excited voice, like a hound's on a red-hot coon trail. It was like two hounds, rather, going wild and about to bring their quarry to bay.

It was no time to argue with one of your best friends who had just saved your life, when you were maybe in even more danger than you had been. But I couldn't keep myself from exploding back at him. "Those are *hounds!* Alexander the Coppersmith wasn't any hound! He was a crossbreed of half a dozen different kinds of dogs!"

Dragonfly was right, though. There were dogs barking, and they were wild with excitement. It sounded as though they were near the creek and were coming fast toward the house where we were.

Right then is when the rifleman swooped down on Crimp the Shrimp—if it was Crimp the Shrimp—and handcuffed him, saying at the same time, "You *would* break into my trailer and steal my air mattress and camp stove, would you! Well, you're going to jail, and I'm going to take you there! Do you hear me! I say—"

He didn't get to finish his sentence, because right then there was a man's very loud voice calling from outside the house, where the hounds were still whooping it up.

"All right, Crimp! We know you're in there! Come on out with your hands up!"

At almost the same second another voice came from somewhere inside the house. "Hey, you guys down there! Give me a break, will you? Get me out of here!"

There was also a pounding noise upstairs. It was Poetry, the barrel-shaped member of the gang, still locked in the attic. He was too big around to get through the hole into the chimney and come down like the rest of us, and he had missed out on all the dangerous fun we'd been having.

Things happened fast after that, and I was in the middle of even more exciting excitement than I had been.

It took only a few minutes to find out that the man outside, ordering our unconscious prisoner to come out with his hands up, was the sheriff. There was a posse with him, and the wild-with-excitement hounds were blood-hounds. They'd been trailing Crimp the Shrimp all day. When the storm struck, the dogs had lost the trail and hadn't found it again until the rain let up. Hounds can't follow a trail when there is a rainstorm to wash away the scent.

The rifleman turned out to be Jake Peters, who lived in the next county in a homemade house trailer. When Crimp the Shrimp had broken in one night that week and stolen his air mattress, a camp stove, and other things, Jake had been so mad that he had gotten himself deputized and started out on a one-man manhunt. The fact that Jake was hard of hearing and hadn't had any sleep for two nights explained quite a few things to my curious mind.

In the middle of the excitement, somebody went upstairs and got Poetry out of his attic jail. When he came down, he was grumpily mumbling something about going on a diet.

And I got a chance to use my first-aid supplies on Crimp the Shrimp, for that's who it turned out our prisoner was. It took me only a little while to put Merthiolate and a bandage on his gashed temple where he had struck the fireplace hearth and also on his arm where it looked as if he'd been scratched by some briers.

I had a few scratches and bruises on my own soot-tarnished self.

A little later, after a lot of explanations and a little advice from the sheriff, and also thanks, and after they had taken down all our names and our addresses, the gang was alone again. We were outside the house and beside the canine cemetery, ready to do what we had come to do in the first place—rebury Alexander the Coppersmith.

The late afternoon sun was casting long shadows across the woods when we finished the work the moles had started under the elderberry bush. Then we went back into the house to get Old Tom the Trapper's musical album.

We took the loose board out of the fireplace where it had fallen, carried it back upstairs, and put it where it had been. We slid the closet's secret panel into place again and took a final look at the tinned supplies. The camp stove and the air mattress were already gone, taken home by the rifleman. And pretty soon we were on our way to Old Man Paddler's cabin.

Anybody watching us would have thought we were an odd-looking gang of boys. Five of us from head to toe were like St. Nicholas had been in "The Night Before Christmas," clothes "all tarnished with ashes and soot."

But in spite of the way we looked and the bruises we all had—especially me—we felt fine. What a story we would have to tell our folks when we got back! And how surprised Old Man Paddler would be to see Tom the Trapper's missing musical album!

First, we washed the shovel and the spade very carefully in the creek, so Old Man Paddler would be pleased we had remembered his final orders. We also washed off most of the ashes and soot from our hands and faces.

"Let me carry the album," Little Jim begged, and Big Jim let him. He also let me carry the shovel and Poetry the spade.

Dragonfly was worried about his cowboy boots being stained, until we got most of the ashes and soot off. It made me feel fine the way he trudged along, not limping even a little bit, even though I was limping a little myself from what had happened to my left big toe on the way down the chimney.

I had a Band-Aid on it, though, and it didn't hurt too much. That Band-Aid would be proof to my folks that I had been at least a half-hero in the big fight to capture Crimp the Shrimp.

Dragonfly was worried about something, though. "I hope your mother has my clothes ready when we get there," he said to me.

It took us only about ten minutes to get to the place where the fallen ponderosa made a bridge across the canyon. There we stopped to think and to remember what had happened there the week before and to take a final look down at the place where Alexander's first grave had been.

"You know what?" Little Jim said just before we got there.

"What?" I asked.

And he answered, "Let's name the place

79

where Alexander saved my life Wildcat Canyon!"

It seemed a good idea, so we quick voted on it, and that became the name of the place where Alexander the Coppersmith had fought a duel to the death with a fierce-fanged, savage-tempered wildcat, saving Little Jim's life by doing it.

"Hear that?" Dragonfly exclaimed all of a sudden. The way he exclaimed it and the excitement in his voice made me think maybe he was hearing Alexander's ghost again.

We all listened, not knowing for sure what to expect to hear.

"Sounds like a windstorm in the woods somewhere! Maybe it's going to rain again. We'd better hurry on home!" his worried voice whined.

It did sound like wind in the woods. But it also sounded as if there had already been a big rainstorm somewhere and Sugar Creek was on a rampage. Yet, I knew we were too far from the creek to be hearing *it*. Besides, we had washed the spade and shovel in the creek only fifteen minutes ago, and Sugar Creek had been only a little higher than usual.

"Flash flood!" Big Jim cried and broke into a run toward the rim of the canyon with the rest of us at his heels.

I saw it the minute I got there and looked down. Far down and down and down, where two or three hours ago there had been a pile of stones marking the grave of Alexander the

Coppersmith, there was now a river of seething, hissing, turbulent water.

"Cloudburst up in the hills somewhere!" Circus said above the noise of the water.

Even though my thoughts were sad, they were also glad as I thought about the nice quiet grave up in Old Tom the Trapper's canine cemetery by the haunted house, where one of the finest dogs in the world was buried. Next week, maybe, we would come back and put up a marker, one that my cousin Wally would be proud of when he came to visit us next summer, if he did—and he probably would.

Well, we couldn't just keep on standing there thinking and feeling sad. We were carrying home a very pleasant surprise for Old Man Paddler.

Little Jim broke into a run ahead of us then, calling back over his shoulder, "Last one there is a cow's tail!" That's when he stumbled. The album flew out of his hand, bursting open. As it fell, there in the quiet of the woods we heard the sweet music box music of "Silent Night."

Dragonfly had been running just behind Little Jim. He cried then with new excitement in his voice. "Look!" he exclaimed. "There's a lot of *money* in it!"

But there wasn't a lot of money in the box. It was *out* of the box. Scattered all over in a little circle of maybe six or seven feet was what looked like hundreds of dollars in very old, extralarge bills—fives, tens, twenties, and also ones and even twos.

Also, lying in a place by itself was a long, yellowish envelope that said on it in shaky handwriting "The Will of Thomas Alexander Bromley."

We quickly gathered up the scattered bills and made them into a little packet. I tied a piece of gauze bandage around them, and as soon as we had them in the album again and the lid closed and fastened—of course, the music shut itself off—we broke into a run for Old Man Paddler's.

This seemed even more important than capturing Crimp the Shrimp.

I won't have room in this story to tell you the rest of what happened that afternoon—not all of what happened at Old Man Paddler's cabin, anyway. But the old man was as pleased as a boy is on Christmas morning when he gets the surprise gift he's been hoping for a whole year that he would get.

We didn't even take time to take an apple apiece from the barrel, but as soon as we could, we went down through the old man's cellar and into the cave and through it. All of us planned to stop at my house first to get Dragonfly's clothes changed. If his mother got to worrying about him and came over to see what had happened to him, he'd be ready.

We'd reached the north road corner and turned east to go the last eighth of a mile to the Collins place, when we saw the Gilberts' car with Dragonfly's mother at the wheel, stopping at our house!

"Quick!" I said to Dragonfly. "Over the fence and through the orchard to the toolshed. Follow me!"

I broke into a run, and the little guy ran after me. If his worrywart mother saw him with soot-tarnished jeans and shirt, even though they were mine, she might start scolding him.

"Hurry!" Dragonfly cried behind me, and I kept on doing it. There was no use letting him get his heart stabbed with sharp words for nothing. "Quick!" I ordered him. "Into the toolshed! I'll run into the house and get your clothes!"

Mom saw and heard me coming and flew into action. I had Dragonfly's just-pressed jeans and shirt in my hand and was out the kitchen door and into the toolshed in a jiffy. And by the time the rest of the gang got there and Mrs. Gilbert was out of the car asking where her boy was, Dragonfly was just opening the toolshed door and coming out, looking like a million dollars in fresh-as-a-daisy clothes.

"You had me worried half sick!" his mother exclaimed to him. "What with the terrible storm! Are you all right?" Then she saw the rest of us, and her eyes flashed from us to him, back again to us, and then to Mom, who with a very innocent face was standing in the kitchen doorway.

Well, it seemed somebody ought to start explaining things. As fast as I could, I let loose about five hundred words explaining Crimp the Shrimp, the rifleman, the bloodhounds, the sheriff's posse, the hole in the chimney, the music box, and especially my very fast descent down the sooty chimney. When I got to the place in the adventure where we had the fight with Crimp the Shrimp, the way I said it made it seem more dangerous than it was.

"We licked him all to smithereens," I finished, looking at Mom to see how clean I was in her mind's eye in spite of so much ashes and soot on my clothes.

For a few fast-talking minutes I had forgotten Dragonfly's problem and was worrying only about myself. That's when, all of a sudden, Dragonfly's mother looked at her son, whose hands and face—like the rest of ours—was as clean as he could make it with Sugar Creek water and no soap. His were as clean as they usually are after an ordinary afternoon with the gang.

I certainly was astonished at what she said to her nice, clean son. "And you, Roy, what were *you* doing while the rest of the boys were being heroes? Where were you when that dangerous criminal was half killing them? Didn't you join in the fight, too? What did you do? Stay up there in the attic, afraid?"

I had already explained that Poetry hadn't come down the chimney because he was shaped like Santa Claus and the opening in the chimney had been too small. But since Poetry and Dragonfly were the only two of us to have clean clothes, she just naturally supposed her son had been a coward and hadn't joined in the battle.

Well, Dragonfly, like any other boy, wanted his mother to think he was important. He jumped in with a few words of his own just as soon as he could knock a hole through his mother's wall of words. He stammered, "I c–c–climbed d–d–down the rope, too, and I t–t–tackled him with b–b–both hands. I didn't get my clothes dirty. I didn't have them on at the t–t–time." He hardly ever stuttered that badly, but you couldn't blame him.

I heard his mother gasp at that, and a mischievous thought came into my mind. "You wouldn't want him to get his clothes all tarnished with ashes and soot, would you, Mrs. Gilbert?"

Maybe I shouldn't have said it, but it was already out, and I knew what I had helped her think, when she exclaimed to Dragonfly, "You mean you *took your clothes off* and went down that chimney stark naked?"

Things had gone far enough and maybe too far, so Mom, who had a good sense of humor, giggled a little, winked at me, and then explained everything to Mrs. Gilbert. In a little while everybody was satisfied.

The day was over—all the adventure and the thrills and the dangerous excitement. Maybe there never would be another day like it in Sugar Creek history.

After a while the rest of the gang went to

their different homes, and only Dragonfly and his mother were left. She seemed very proud of her son, who had been the real hero in the capture of Crimp the Shrimp.

A little later, when they were on their way to their car to go home to supper, I heard her say to him, "You even kept your new boots nice and clean. A little polish and they'll look just like new for your trip to the Rockies."

I ran after them to get the gate open for Mrs. Gilbert, as a boy is supposed to do for a lady, and I quickly whispered to Dragonfly, "Straighten your hat a little. The brim's got a twist in it. You want *it* to look just right for your trip to the Rockies, too."

He grinned at me and whispered back, "My heel doesn't hurt a bit. Not even a little bit."

As their car moved away and went whirring up the road, I turned and hurried over to the rope swing. I got on, stood up, and pumped myself higher and higher and higher until I could see, over the rim of the hill, the reflection of the sun on the top of the Gilberts' car on its way to their house.

I looked across the road then to where Dragonfly had been standing a long time ago. It seemed long ago, anyway. And I remembered hearing him say, "I'm going to ride on the longest chairlift in the world. Clear up to the top of Ajax Mountain!"

Right then my dream thoughts were interrupted by Mom's cheerful voice sailing out across the lawn. "Bill! Come on in! I want you to sample a piece of fresh apple pie just before you take a bath and change your clothes!"

Even though, as you already know, one of my pet peeves is to have my dream thoughts interrupted, my *most* pet peeve is to be asked to take a bath when I have already planned to take one without being asked.

But it seemed Mom's idea was a good one, so I slowed myself down as fast as I could, swung out of the swing—letting the old cat take all the time it wanted to finish dying—and was off on a gallop past the plum tree toward the house, calling out in a loud voice for all the world to hear, "Hi-yo, Silver!"

The *Sugar Creek Gang* Series: